Tales of Murder and Mayhem

TALES OF MURDER AND MAYHEM

Marc Trop

authorHOUSE®

AuthorHouse™
1663 Liberty Drive
Bloomington, IN 47403
www.authorhouse.com
Phone: 1-800-839-8640

First published by AuthorHouse   09/22/2011

ISBN: 978-1-4670-2599-7 (sc)
ISBN: 978-1-4670-2600-0 (ebk)

Library of Congress Control Number: 2011915824

Printed in the United States of America

Any people depicted in stock imagery provided by Thinkstock are models, and such images are being used for illustrative purposes only.
Certain stock imagery © Thinkstock.

This book is printed on acid-free paper.

CONTENTS

ACKNOWLEDGMENT

I wish to express my thanks to my wife, Dr. Forough Trop for her help in preparing my manuscript. and to my son, Robert Trop and Murray Bromberg, my colleague, for their advice and suggestions in bringing my stories to print.

INTRODUCTION

Crime stories have always rated highly as a topic in literature. The bible itself in the first book of Genesis tells a tale of Fraticide. The bible's first couple, Adam and Eve, give birth to two sons. In the King James version of the bible, their older son Cain in a fit of jealously, murders his brother Abel. In chapter 4, we also get the first attempt at an alibi when as we read, "And the Lord said unto Cain, Where is Abel thy brother? And he said, I know not: Am I my brother's keeper?" There you have it. Murder and lying found in an early story in the bible.

It took centuries before crime fiction became very popular. In the United States, Edgar Allan Poe is considered the pioneer writer in making detective fiction popular.

In writing about crime, a decision must be made whether to write true crime or fiction. It is my belief that crime fiction should read like a true story. These stories will not have super heroes leaping over buildings or deflecting bullets with their bodies. There are no science fiction characters here.

You will not meet zombies or vampires. The criminals here could be like your neighbors.

My hope is that reading these tales will arouse your interest and leave you satisfied to have read these stories. ENJOY!

THE LONE TERRORIST

"the first thing we do, let's kill all the lawyers." This famous line written by Shakespeare is often quoted by people trying to be funny who know that I'm a lawyer. One of the strange things about the law profession is that many people like to say negative things about lawyers without having any knowledge about how lawyers work. As for Shakespeare's line, I'll give you odds these people never read Shakespeare and if they did they would not understand his meaning. If you know Shakespeare, he was referring to the bad guys who wanted to get rid of the lawyers because the lawyers were the good guys opposing criminals. Another comment, "You're a criminal lawyer. How many crimes have you committed?"

Ha. Ha. Big joke. Everybody gets a laugh from the joke. Unless you're a lawyer.

My name is Joshua Blaine. I have a modest office, actually a storefront in a busy commercial area in a small state. I wanted to get away from the atmosphere of a big city so I figured a small state would suit me better. Years ago, I would probably be called a country lawyer, out to help clients with minor problems.

My aim is to treat people with decency and to leave them satisfied with my assistance. When I graduated from law school, I began working at a large law firm. The salary was exceptionally high for a beginner, but I hated the work. There was constant pressure to win cases at all costs, even if the merit wasn't there. In addition, I was expected to bring new clients in or else I was looked upon as a failure.

There was little satisfaction in that position. I left the job after a short period. I then was hired at the county prosecutor's office. Here again, there was little joy in working at that office. The main purpose of that office was to win convictions and put people in prison. I'm not a "bleeding heart" and I do believe many criminals need to be incarcerated. But there needs to be some compassion beyond conviction when the guilty are sentenced. Minor first-time offenders deserve some consideration, especially when there are mitigating circumstances. I was not happy with the operation in the prosecutor's office and finally decided to leave and work as a solo practitioner. You don't get rich, but at least you are your own master and there is a greater level of contentment with your work. The only liability is sometimes you wonder about the importance of cases that come to you. After spending years in law school you ask yourself if all that study was worth it. Also, what important difference was I making in the lives of clients? Minor civil cases are not life or death issues. And so I felt. That is until the case of the lone terrorist came into my life.

Leaving a practice in a big city, I began work as a solo practitioner in a small state. I moved to Delaware where I opened a storefront office. Delaware has one interesting distinction. It was the first state to ratify the constitution. It's also one of the smallest states in the country. I figured a small state would free me from the hassle found in a big state. When things are real slow, I stand in the doorway and watch the parade of people walking by. I find this relaxing when there is little to do. I have one secretary who runs the office and even offers advice, sometimes on legal matters even though she is not a lawyer. She is especially good at sizing up people. If I had to describe her I would say she has a lot of common sense and is street smart. She is old enough to be my mother and I accept her as a kind of mother hen and a positive addition to the office.

The client came in off the street, without an appointment, and was met by Gertie, my office secretary who also acts as a receptionist. Gertie greets people and fills out a standard form which tells me the person's name and address and if possible she writes what the person wants a lawyer to do. Her summary tells me in a word or two what the issue is. For example, she might write 'Civil/Matrimonial' or 'Criminal' to give me an idea what the issue might be. Gertie will often give me a thumbs up signal if she likes the person. How she makes such a judgment without knowing anything about the person amazes me because she is usually right in her evaluations. The client was ushered into my office with a thumbs up sign by Gertie. I was impressed. She was dressed conservatively, and she wore a dark business suit of designer origin. You could see she was not wearing what I call clothes from discount stores. Her skirt just reached her knees and her voice was soft and the thing that told me a lot about her was how well she spoke correct English. You can tell a lot about a person by how well he or she speaks English. A person can try to act above her class, but you can tell a lot by the use of words like "ain't" "you was instead of you were" "gonna instead of going to" "da for the" and lots of other words that give them away. With the thumbs up from Gertie and my own evaluation, I had a positive feeling about her. Her name was Jean Timpson and she did not seem happy. And why not?

People usually don't need a lawyer unless there is a problem.

I began with my usual opening. "How do you do. Please have a seat. I'm Joshua Blaine. Please tell me what your problem is."

She began: "Please excuse me if get emotional. It's about my husband. I believe he was murdered.

The police say he committed suicide. That's not possible. My husband would never commit suicide. It just can't be true. They say he jumped to his death off a tall building. He would never do that."

"I'm sorry about your loss. But, how can I help you?"

" I want to find out who killed him, that is who pushed or threw him off the roof."

"I need to explain a few things. If your husband was murdered, then it is a criminal matter. While a lawyer in almost all matters decides which side to represent, there is no choice in criminal cases.

The only side in criminal cases for lawyers is the defense side. The other side is the prosecution.

The prosecutor is often called the District Attorney, or the state's attorney, or the prosecutor. They try to find you guilty. The defense side tries to find you innocent. Defense lawyers don't go around chasing criminals. That only happens in the movies. But let me see if I can offer some help. You should know that a murder committed by throwing someone off a roof is a very difficult crime to solve because there is no weapon involved. Let me try to offer some assistance. First, a few questions. Don't be offended by my questions even though they may be very sensitive. I assume there was no suicide note."

"Absolutely not."

"Did he have any enemies? Anyone who might want him dead."

"None."

"What did he do for a living?"

"He taught in a high school."

"Might there be some student who was angry over a grade or something?"

"No. He was one of the most popular teachers in the school. He was an absolutely gentle person."

"Did he have any financial problems?"

"None. We weren't rich, but we both worked as teachers, paid all our bills on time, and had no outstanding large bills to worry about."

"I have to ask you. Is there any chance that he was having an affair?"

"No. No. We were in a completely happy marriage. If you knew him you would never ask such a question. That's what makes this so unlikely. As far as I'm concerned, he was one in a million."

"What else can you tell me about him?"

"He was very normal. He loved to watch baseball on television. He even collected baseball cards."

"I have some police contacts and I'll keep my eyes open. I'll let you know if I come up with anything."

"Is there any charge for this visit?"

"No, None."

She left the office rather unhappily. I didn't expect anything to develop from this problem and I just put the folder with a brief summary on Gertie's out-basket to be filed away. Not all cases have a happy ending like the movies. Sadly, I thought that was the end of the case. Little did I know.

His name was Richard Worcester. At an early age he was trouble. In elementary school he often acted as a bully picking on weaker students. He argued with teachers and sometimes made physical threats against others. He was diagnosed as having bipolar disorder. When he reached high school he did some research on his last name. A U.S. Supreme Court case known as Worcester v. Georgia in 1832 caught his attention. Worcester was a case that involved the state of Georgia and the sovereignty of the Cherokee Indian Nation. Worcester was a missionary working among the Cherokees. He was arrested and jailed by the state of Georgia for violating a prohibition against his work in helping the Indians.

Although the Supreme Court sided with Worcester, President Jackson refused to enforce the decision. The decision supported an act of Congress known as the Indian Removal Act. Georgia was free to force the Cherokees to give up their land and move west to Oklahoma. The forced removal of the Cherokees was known as the Trail of Tears. Thousands of Indians died on the march west. It was also called the Trail of Death. Richard Worcester was delusional and believed he was a descendent of Worcester. Thus, he began to hate the United States because he believed the government had unfairly punished his ancestor.

He was a natural born American, but as he grew older his grudge and hatred against fellow Americans and the United States grew. As he saw it, everything the United States did was bad, and he lamented the fact that the American Revolution had succeeded. He felt we would have been better off if the colonies had remained part of Great Britain. His hatred began as early as his days in school. He also resented the fact that he did not get higher grades and he blamed the system and the government that was in charge of his public education. To his thinking, the requirement for mandatory education was an invasion of his freedom. In addition, he was once assaulted and robbed. When the assailant was caught and brought to trial, the only penalty imposed by the court was probation. He was angry over that decision. He believed the government could not be trusted to protect innocent victims like himself.

When the World Trade Center was destroyed on September 11, 2001, he felt a satisfaction and was glad it happened.

That event also created a purpose and a destiny for his life. He would become a Jihadist and kill as many Americans as possible. He had to create a plan that would ensure success.

He decided that being a suicide bomber was stupid. If you killed yourself, you could no longer continue with your destiny.

He did some research on serial killers. First there was Jack the Ripper. He murdered prostitutes in The White Chapel district of London in 1888. The area was a slum district and he confined the murders to the same area and used the same method which consisted of using a knife as a weapon. He was never caught and the case remained unsolved, probably forever.

In recent times there was the so-called Zodiac killer. The murders took place in northern California in the late 1960's and early 1970's. Again the murderer was never caught and the case remained unsolved. Another serial killer was Jeffrey Dahmer. He confined himself to the area around Milwaukee, Wisconsin.

Around 17 known murders are attributed to him. He was caught and was imprisoned for life.

Finally, there was David Berkowitz, also known as Son of Sam. He killed 6 or 7 people in the New York City area. He was caught and imprisoned for life. Based on these facts, the terrorist worked out a plan as follows:

1. Any mass killing would bring media attention to an extreme and bring the full force of the police to try to catch him. Therefore, each killing would involve one victim at a time.
2. He knew the police always looked for a motive and so it was imperative for him to keep any motive difficult to determine.
3. The location of each killing would be far removed from each other.
4. Serial killers usually used the same method to kill people. His plan would rely on a different method for every killing.

He looked over his plan and a smile of satisfaction crossed his lips.

Let the Jihad begin!

The terrorist headed for Pennsylvania. He rented a car and began to drive into an area that might provide a suitable target for his next victim. He consulted a travel guide and an idea came to him. It would be wonderful to kill a professor working at a law school. In his mind the professors were responsible for educating lawyers who were to blame for the excessive awards in civil suits that he read about in newspapers and heard about on various talk shows. He faulted the lawyers for the high cost of insurance. Never mind if an award was merited or if not could be reduced by a judge or an appeals court. He stopped at a coffee shop adjacent to a law school and walked in and ordered a cup of coffee. A pile of student newspapers were stacked on a table as free handouts. He took one and browsed through the pages. There was an interesting ad about a lecture being given by a Professor Thomas on the topic of the successful influence of capitalism in providing a high standard of living in the United States. The lecture was free for the public. It looked like a wonderful opportunity for his mission.

A parking lot for students and faculty was available across the road from the campus. He parked his car in the lot. Since the killing of 12 students and one teacher on campus in the Columbine High School massacre in Colorado there was heightened security at schools in the United States. The entire campus was surrounded by an eight foot chain-link fence and most cars were not allowed to drive through the entrance. Every car had to enter through a security checkpoint at the main entrance. He was able to walk through the checkpoint without difficulty. He followed signs directing him to the auditorium where the lecture was taking place. He took a seat near the front row. When the professor approached the dais he eyed him carefully to make sure the professor's face would make a permanent impression on his brain. When the lecture was finished, he went to his car and waited until he was able to spot the professor and watched him as he drove out of the parking lot. He made sure to notice the make of the car, its color and the license plate number. He wrote the information carefully in his notepad.

The next day he parked his car in the vicinity where the professor had parked the day before. He knew that most people parked in the same general area. Eventually he saw the professor parking his car near where he was parked and he watched and waited. When he was in the army he had been trained as a demolitions expert.

He was fully qualified and prepared to carry out his jihad. He had brought his explosives with him and without being seen, he surreptitiously planted the explosive under the professor's car so that it would detonate when the car started.

Hours later, the professor entered his car and started the motor. The explosion was loud and devastating. The professor was killed instantly. The terrorist had succeeded.

The phone rang at 11 P.M. at Jason's apartment. An apprehensive feeling came over him.

When someone called late at night it usually meant bad news. Why else would someone call at such a late hour?

He picked up the receiver and answered hello.

"Hi, it's Robert."

Robert was a classmate and close friend from law school.

"I have some bad news. You probably haven't heard about it yet."

"What's up?"

"Professor Thomas has been killed. Someone planted a bomb under his car and apparently it exploded and killed him instantly."

Professor Thomas had been a confidant and a mentor to Joshua. He was very close to him.

Robert continued: "There is going to be a service for him tomorrow. I'm sure you want to be there."

"Of course."

Robert provided the relevant information about time and place.

The next day Joshua arrived at the service. A large crowd of friends, relatives, present and former students filled the room.

A family member spoke about how beloved the professor had been.

A religious leader read the Lord's Prayer.

A close friend spoke about the kind of person the professor had been. He had no enemies. It was hard to understand why someone would want to kill him.

As Joshua listened to all the kind words it reminded him of the way Jean Timpson spoke about her husband. A thought crossed his mind.

What if the same person had committed both crimes? No! That was too far-fetched. States apart for the crime. Different modus operandi. Forget it.

He left the service with a heavy heart. It would be a long time before he realized how close he had come to the truth.

New Jersey was the next state to be targeted by the terrorist. He drove there without any idea about who his next victim would be. Somehow he believed an inspiration from God would come to him and he would know exactly where, when, and how to commit his next jihad. He came into a large city and drove around aimlessly until he noticed a crowd of people lining up to go into a movie theatre.

The idea came to him as he knew it would. First, he would kill a woman. Nothing like equal rights as far as his next victim being a woman instead of a man. Second, he would strike at night when there would be less chance of being observed.

He waited until the last showing of the movie was over. He needed to find a woman who was leaving by herself and walking in a secluded area. The plan was to follow her in his car, park ahead of her, seize her as she passed by, drag her into the car, drive to a secluded area and then take his next step.

For several nights he waited and watched, but there was no suitable target. He was getting frustrated.

But he had patience and did not give up easily. Finally after several nights a possible victim appeared. A rush of excitement came over him. It was about midnight. She appeared to be in her twenties. Slim, about 5'3". Perfect! She would not be able to offer much resistance.

He debated whether to first have sex with his prisoner. He remembered having sex in the first car he owned while a teen-ager. The thought excited him. While fantasizing he remembered those days and sex in the back seat. His girl friend would play a game of baseball with him that he had invented. Let's play baseball he would suggest. His date had several options. They would start at first base. First base was for hugging and kissing. Then came second base which consisted of masturbation. Third base was for oral sex. Home plate, a home run, going all the way with intercourse. At any base his date could ask for a rain check and end the lovemaking.

Now there would be no rain checks and no options. These thoughts helped him pass the time as he waited. It was close to midnight. The streets were deserted. He followed behind her in his car.

Feeling safe he drove ahead of her, parked the car and went to the backseat, and quietly left the back door ajar to avoid any noise when he would swing the door open. He crouched below the window so that he would not be noticed. She came abreast of the car. As she passed alongside, he opened the door and leaped out behind her, grabbed her by putting his arm around her neck and dragged her into the car. He was getting excited and felt the beginning of an erection. He warned her to remain quiet and told her she would not be hurt if she didn't scream for help. He flashed a box cutter before her face.

He covered her eyes with a hand towel and pulled down his pants and underwear. He told her to open her mouth and attempted to put his penis in her mouth. But he had lost his erection and felt frustrated. Perhaps he needed intercourse. He pulled her skirt up and pulled down her panties. She yelled for him to stop but he slapped her face hard across the cheek several times.

"Don't resist and you won't get hurt." He tried to penetrate into her vagina but he had no erection and she was not lubricated. "Please let me go." she begged. "Sure." he answered. Instead he quickly used his box cutter and slit her throat and made sure her life was over. Then he drove to a secluded area and threw her body between two parked cars.

New Jersey was successful. There was one less American to worry about.

The next target for the terrorist was the state of Georgia. He decided the method for murder would involve the use of poison. The use of poison presented four problems that needed to be resolved. They included the following:

1. What poison should he use?
2. Where should the poison be used?
3. Who should be his next victim?
4. How would he get his victim to take the poison?

Traveling to Georgia was the easy part. He went to the railroad station and purchased a ticket to Atlanta. It was easy to buy a ticket and board the train. There was no security check. He thought that in some future time it would be easy to explode a bomb in the passenger car of a train and kill many people, but that was not in his plan for now.

While traveling to Atlanta, he began to organize his thoughts for his operation. Upon arriving at his destination, he found a gardening outlet store. He asked a salesclerk for an insecticide that could be used to kill rats. He said rats had invaded his property and he needed some kind of arsenic or cyanide that would be deadly. He needed a liquid or powder to do the job.

The salesclerk provided a liquid based poison.

There is a long history about using poison to kill people. In ancient and medieval times poison was often used to kill enemies. The usual techniques involved mixing the poison into food or wine. In fact many prominent political leaders would use tasters to test the safety of their wine or food because they were afraid of being poisoned.

The terrorist made the purchase and then found a pharmacy where he purchased a syringe.

He had his plan all worked out. He found a restaurant where there was a buffet table. Customers served themselves and could go back as often as they liked. He sat down at a corner booth and made sure there was no person that could look over his shoulder. He took a tray and headed to a section where the desserts were offered. He placed a chocolate cake with colored sprinkles on his tray. He felt that would appeal to a child. A child would be less suspicious about the food. He sat down in the booth with the tray of chocolate. He took the syringe that had been filled with the poison and injected the liquid into the cake. He then took the cake back to the dessert table and made sure not to be observed.

He quickly put the dish with the cake back on the table. Then he left the restaurant and waited outside.

He did not need to wait too long.

After a short period, he heard the siren of an ambulance approach the restaurant. He was not certain about success. Still he was satisfied that he had done some harm. He saw a couple leave in tears.

He asked a person leaving the restaurant what had happened.

"A child died from some kind of food poisoning."

He had his answer. Success again.

The terrorist left Georgia and headed to Connecticut. He took the Amtrak train and arrived at his destination without any problems. He made sure to reach a large city where his plan could continue safely. He went to a hardware store and purchased a hammer.

After making inquiries, he took a bus to a mall. He went to a fairly remote parking area and selected a car for his next deed. He made sure there were no witnesses nearby. With the hammer, he quickly punched the window out so that he could open the door on the driver's side.

Inside the car, he was able to cross the wires and start the motor. Then he drove to a street where pedestrians were walking and window shopping. He saw an elderly man crossing the street in his path.

Stepping on the gas pedal, he reached full speed in a few moments. With deliberate aim he struck the old man and knocked him to the ground. The old man didn't have a chance to escape the collision.

He was dead on contact.

The terrorist sped to the corner, made a turn and drove away. He reached a quiet street, got out of the car, and walked away. Success again! Everything was going well.

The police arrived at the scene. It looked like a typical hit and run accident. The officer in his initial report marked it down as negligent homicide.

Shortly thereafter the abandoned car was found and after checking the license plate the police knew that the car had been stolen.

Why would someone steal a car, kill an elderly man crossing the street and then abandon the car?

Obviously it was an intentional collision. The police report was then modified. The word negligent was crossed out. Now the report was listed as criminal homicide. But what was the motive? That seemed a mystery.

Only the terrorist knew what the motive was. And once again, the jihad was going exactly as planned.

The next target was Massachusetts. Massachusetts is the state that is directly north of Connecticut.

Therefore it was a short trip and the best way to travel there was to take a bus. It was a simple matter to purchase a ticket and once again he thought how easy it would be for a suicide bomber to board a bus and kill many passengers with a bomb. There was absolutely no security check to worry about. Still that was not part of his plan for now. He had to stay alive in order to continue with the jihad.

He was not exactly sure about the specific technique he would use. He was confident that the trip would enable him to think and plan. Surely something would come to his mind. The bus was filled to capacity and the terrorist settled in his seat. He could hear the conversation between a couple seated nearby. They were tourists returning from a vacation. They had been on a cruise and they discussed the enjoyment they had at sea. The terrorist listened carefully and suddenly an idea came to him. Why not take a cruise? Surely there would be an opportunity to throw someone overboard.

And just like that the idea came to him. The bus arrived in Boston and many passengers got off including the terrorist. He checked into a room at a nearby motel. He took a shower, had a nap and felt invigorated. He consulted the yellow pages of a phone book and looked up cruises.

He wanted to take a cruise on a one day round trip. In addition, he looked for trip that was for singles.

It would be important to throw someone overboard who was not traveling with anyone. It would be less likely that a lone traveler was missing.

He found an ad for one day cruises for singles. Great! He took a cab to the port and found a booth where tickets were sold for the trip. With the ticket he boarded the boat and after leaving port, he mingled with the passengers. The cruise included many activities. There was a lot of food and alcoholic drinks available in various parts of the boat. It was like one big party. As darkness approached he circled around the ship. He kept close to the railings. He made several trips around the ship. So far nothing seemed to develop that would meet his needs. He was getting frustrated. Maybe this was not such a good idea. Then his fortune changed. He saw a young woman, probably in her twenties, wandering near the railing. Her walk was not steady. He was not sure if she had too much to drink or whether the motion of the ship was making her wobble as she walked. In any event, he quickly walked behind her. He had armed himself with a small hammer. Making sure there were no witnesses, he struck her from behind with full force. She was knocked unconscious immediately. He then used his strength to quickly throw her overboard. As he expected, she was not missed by anyone. When the ship docked, a friend waited to greet the victim.

After a long wait, the victim's friend notified the office about her concern.

The ship's captain was called into the office. He knew nothing about the disappearance. After making several inquiries, the thinking was that she may have jumped overboard and committed suicide. There was no thought about a homicide. The Boston papers did give it some publicity.

The headline read: "Was it Murder or Suicide? Who Knows?"

The terrorist was satisfied. Another victim. All was going well.

The terrorist left Massachusetts and headed for Maryland. He took the bus after purchasing a ticket for Baltimore, the capital of Maryland. After arriving at his destination, he exited the bus and began walking along a main street. He found a discount clothing store and entered. After looking over the merchandise, he found what he was looking for.

He selected some overalls and tried them on. The fit was good enough for his purpose. He could easily be taken for a handyman. He purchased the item by paying cash. He then walked along the main street until he found a hardware store. He purchased a strong piece of rope, about two feet in length.

Next he purchased a spray gun insecticide. He could pass for a maintenance worker.

He found an apartment building, rang a bell at random in order to get a response that enabled him to enter the building. He walked to the first floor and rang a bell at the first apartment he saw. No response. Obviously, there was no person at home. He came to a second door. He put his ear to the door and could hear voices coming from within. No good! He needed to find an apartment with only one person at home.

The third try looked good. An elderly lady opened the door.

"The landlord sent me. I need to spray the corners and under the bed in order to protect against insects around your apartment.

"I'm glad you are here." she said.

He followed her into the apartment. He was sure she was alone. He grabbed her from behind and struck her with his hammer. He tied the rope to an overhead fixture. Then he carried her to a chair that he placed under the fixture. He lifted her to the chair. She was small and light of weight.

Easily done! He put her in a standing position on the chair and quickly kicked the chair out from her legs. The hanging was successful. She was dead in a few minutes. He congratulated himself on his ingenuity. The plan was working extremely well.

The next day the papers carried the story in the main section. Neighbors were interviewed.

Everyone was shocked. This was no suicide. The press quoted several people who knew her. A common remark described her as a gentle kind person. She had no enemies. Why would anyone do such a terrible thing?

Shocking! Shocking! This was a frequent word heard as neighbors gathered to discuss the tragedy.

Only the terrorist was not shocked.

Next on the terrorist's target list was South Carolina. He purchased a ticket at the train station for Columbia, South Carolina. Columbia was the capital city and he believed it would not be difficult to go ahead with his plan in a large city. In order to continue using different methods for murder, it was necessary to use a weapon that he had kept from his time in the armed service.

He had also served as a medic in the service and was issued a standard M 1911 pistol. When he neared discharge, he had gone on a three day pass. He took the pistol with him off the base. In those days there was little check on weapons for military personnel going on a legitimate leave. It was easy to leave the base without any control against weapons.

He had kept the gun in a dresser drawer for many years. Now it was time to put the weapon to use.

He was glad he had kept the pistol. With the use of a pistol he could easily kill a suitable victim.

He walked through the streets and reached a seedy part of town. There were some homeless people sleeping in alleys. He stopped at a liquor store and purchased a bottle of cheap wine.

He came to a church and noticed a homeless man who appeared to be half awake lying on the sidewalk. Obviously, he had been drinking since a bottle of wine was at his feet. The terrorist approached the man and opened the bottle of wine that he had purchased. He offered the bottle to the wino. The man eagerly took it and began drinking. The terrorist made sure he was not observed.

He quickly took out his gun and put it to the man's head. One quick shot was all he needed to finish his purpose. Another success to chalk up as the jihad continued.

Next on his list was New Hampshire. New Hampshire was the ninth state to ratify the United States Constitution.

Since nine states were needed to approve and establish the present government, the state was proud of the role it played when it ratified the constitution on June 21, 1788. The terrorist was not aware of the significance of New Hampshire's role in the ratification process.

He purchased a ticket for a bus trip to Concord, New Hampshire. When he arrived at Concord, he rented a car at an auto rental agency. He drove outside the city and discovered the state had large rural areas. The next murder was beginning to develop in his mind. He drove back to the city and located a bookstore that sold religious books. He purchased several bibles and a briefcase.

He went to a local library and received permission to use a computer. He surfed the internet and typed:

"Widow's Club, Concord." A list provided several churches that had widow's clubs listed. The churches also provided phone numbers and addresses of the churches. He called several churches.

One church had a widows' club. He called and asked when the club met. When he found a suitable time for his objective, he asked for driving directions to the church. The club met on Sunday after services. He would have to wait a few days to accomplish his purpose. He rented a room in a cheap motel and waited. On Sunday he drove to the church, parked the car and watched to see who was coming out when services ended. After services, a crowd of churchgoers exited. He knew the widow's club would meet after services. There would probably be a period for socialization and refreshments.

He waited patiently. After about two hours a group of elderly women began to exit. Some climbed into the same car, obviously car pooling. When he saw an elderly woman drive off by herself, he followed discreetly. She drove to her home, in a rural area, parked the car in the driveway, and entered her house. The terrorist parked his car a short distance away. It couldn't be better. There was little chance that he would be observed.

He rang the doorbell. She opened the door slightly and seemed hesitant.

"Hello. I'm selling bibles at a deep discount. They are brand new." he said.

She opened the door and let him enter. Once inside, he made sure she was alone. Then he suddenly punched her several times and made sure she was unconscious.

She was elderly, not too strong and an easy conquest. He took a lighter and began to use the flame to torch several parts of the room. He lit the curtains, the bedcovers, the towels in the bathroom and various magazines and books that he found in the den. He stayed a few minutes to make sure the fire would gain in strength. He made sure all windows were shut tight and the doors were firmly closed.

The smoke was entering a deadly stage. He quickly exited. No one saw him. He sat in the car and watched until the flames became visible. The house was quickly burning down. He drove away and congratulated himself on his cleverness.

This venture was becoming fun to carry out.

The terrorist had kept the rented car and decided to drive to Virginia. He felt a special thrill about committing murder in Virginia because the state abutted Washington D.C. Being close to the capital of the United States would be especially satisfying as he carried out his plan. As usual, he had no specific target in mind. He was confident that God was on his side and a suitable victim would appear.

It took several days to reach Virginia. On the way he stopped overnight at cheap motels and thought about the method for murder that he would use. When he reached Virginia, he drove around in search of a target.

As he drove in a suburban area a car driven by a young person suddenly cut in front of him.

Son of a bitch he mumbled to himself. He decided to follow the car that had cut him off.

He was filled with road rage. When the car turned into a quiet and deserted street he drove in front of the other car forcing it to pull over to the curb.

He got out of his car and approached the other driver who remained in his seat. When the driver pulled his window down he shouted. "You cut me off."

"I'm sorry, I didn't mean it." apologized the young man.

The terrorist thought about using his revolver to shoot him in the head and finish him off.

But it was daylight and the sound of the gun might prevent a clean getaway. Despite his road rage, he would let the incident pass by.

The young man didn't know how fortunate he was.

The terrorist had kept the bibles that he had used in New Hampshire. Now he went door to door posing as a bible salesman. Some people let him in but they were not suitable for his mission.

Some were not home alone, other doors were opened by men who appeared capable of too much resistance. Finally, a girl about sixteen years of age opened the door. He knew she would not be interested in buying a bible. He used a ruse to get into the house.

"I'm looking for Mary Syms. Does she live here?" he asked.

"No. You must have the wrong address." she answered.

"Oh, I'm so sorry." he said in a very polite manner. "I sell bibles and she had called my office because she said she might be interested in buying one."

He showed her the bibles that he carried in his briefcase.

" Might your parents be interested in buying a bible? I can leave a copy with you. It's a great buy.

No obligation to pay for it now."

She thought for a moment and finally agreed to take a bible.

"By the way, I'm a little embarrassed to ask but could I use your bathroom for a moment"

She let him in and pointed to the location of the bathroom.

He passed the kitchen and noticed some silverware on a table, including a knife.

He grabbed the knife and made sure she was alone.

Then he grabbed her and flung her to the floor. He flashed the knife and threatened to use it if she screamed. He grabbed her throat with both hands and began choking her. He was strong and she was unable to call for help. He made sure her life was over.

He left the house and drove off ready for his next target.

Crimes are solved in various ways. Often unexpected events occur that open doors to new clues that help to unravel the mystery protecting a criminal. The most obvious way to catch a criminal is when a crime is caught in the act. In modern times forensic evidence like DNA and video cameras have played a leading role in helping police solve a crime. Criminals, often feeling confident, like to boast about their exploits and tell friends about outwitting the police.

Sometimes, criminals in prison talk to fellow inmates about their deeds.

The fellow inmates often come forward with the information seeking a deal that will lessen their incarceration. In the present case a totally unexpected occurrence began to give Joshua some suspicions about a serial killer.

Joshua Blaine sat in his office in the late afternoon looking over a case file concerning a claim of negligence. A woman had been bitten severely by a dog and had required medical attention. He had done the research to prepare his case. He knew the local ordinance permitted no defense if the attacking dog was not on a leash. In addition, if the dog had shown a propensity to bite, liability would attach. Certain dogs like Pit Bulls, Dobermans, German Shepherds, and Rottweilers, if provoked or trained to attack, would bite humans. Joshua was debating whether to advise his client to accept a settlement or to take a chance by going to trial.

The decision was up to the client, but the lawyer could offer advice regarding which option to take.

Joshua glanced at his calendar and saw that Gertie had penciled an appointment with Jean Timpson for that afternoon. In addition, he had a dinner invite for that evening from his sister who was divorced and lived nearby. He looked forward to visiting his sister and her 10 year old son. The intercom flashed signaling a call from Gertie.

He pressed the key which brought Gertie on his line.

"Yes. What is it? He asked.

"Miss Timpson is here."

"Well, show her in Gertie. Show her in."

The door opened to his inner office and Jean Timpson entered. She looked quite different in comparison to her initial visit. She wore a brightly colored blouse, a tan skirt, her hair had been cut short, and she appeared quite attractive.

He thought she was the kind of woman he would like to date. Perhaps he could ask her out to dinner.

No. He had a dinner date at his sister's, and besides it was not ethical for a lawyer to date a client.

He greeted her and asked what was on her mind.

"I was wondering if you had heard anything about my husband."

He wondered if there was any significance to the fact that she did not refer to her husband as her late husband.

"I haven't heard anything. I think the police have put it away in the cold case file."

What he said was true, but he did not say that he had not done any investigation into the matter. The case had been filed away by his office as a cold case and he thought that would be the end of the matter. He felt some guilt over his lack of diligence in handling the case.

The Code of Professional Responsibility mandated attorneys to represent clients zealously.

That meant doing his very best for his client. This he had not done.

He told her not to give up. He said he felt confident that something would turn up.

"Let me ask you something. What was he doing in that building where the tragedy occurred?"

"I believe he went there to buy some baseball cards. I know he put an ad in the paper saying he was interested in buying cards."

"Is there anything else that might be of help to me?"

"I can't think of anything."

"I promise to keep you informed." He said.

When she left, he rang for Gertie to come in.

When Gertie came he spoke to her.

"I want you to do some research. Get me a list of unsolved murders in the last two months that seem to have no motive behind the killings, especially cases that involve someone going off a high elevation."

"Is this related to the Timpson case?"

"Yes, it is."

"I'll do my best."

About three hours later Gertie came into his office telling Joshua she had a list for him.

"That was fast." said Joshua.

"It's easy using the computer. I was able to get police reports and newspaper accounts of various murders. I limited my search to the east coast."

Joshua looked at the list Gertie had prepared.

The heading read:

MODUS OPERANDI	LOCATION BY STATE
1. Suicide or homicide	Delaware (Off building)
2. Car Bomb	Pennsylvania
3. Rape and throat cut	New Jersey
4. Poison	Georgia
5. Hit and Run by car	Connecticut
6. Drowning off Cruise Ship	Massachusetts
7. Hanging	Maryland

8. Gunshot	South Carolina
9. House Fire	New Hampshire
10. Strangling	Virginia

As Joshua looked over the list, Gertie asked: "What does it mean?"

"I'm not sure. We may have a serial killer. The police work on an acronym known as 'MOM'. It stands for motive, opportunity, and means. What I find more meaningful is something I call the pattern. Most serial killers operate on some paradigm. If you can solve the paradigm, it will go a long way to help catch the criminal. I need to think about this list and hope something will help my brain to come up with a clue."

He studied the list several times but it still was an enigma to him. Finally it was getting late and he was hungry. He remembered the dinner date at his sister's house. Gertie had left for the day.

He locked the office and drove to his sister's house.

The main course was spaghetti and turkey meatballs. His sister knew that he did not eat animal products. Turkey was okay. She had prepared one of his favorites. After dinner, they went to the living room for some after dinner conversation. His nephew went to his study to work on a report for his social studies class. When the report was finished, he asked his uncle to look it over. Joshua often helped his nephew by making suggestions and corrections on school reports.

The cover sheet on the report was titled: "Ratifying the Constitution" The writing was very professional. Joshua asked his nephew how he had written the report. The writing was beyond a ten year old student's ability. His nephew said: "I looked up each of the original thirteen states. Then I copied information about each state from the encyclopedia. Joshua looked at the table of contents that his nephew had prepared. It listed each state as follows:

1. Delaware
2. Pennsylvania
3. New Jersey

4. Georgia
5. Connecticut
6. Massachusetts
7. Maryland
8. South Carolina
9. New Hampshire
10. Virginia
11. New York
12. North Carolina
13. Rhode Island

Joshua didn't want to discourage his nephew so he offered some praise. He told his nephew that it was well organized and indicated a good effort. But he had to point out that copying from another source should not be done unless credit was given to the source of the information.

He explained the need for footnotes and how it was used. He wondered if he was going too deep for a ten year old. Still it couldn't hurt to teach his nephew something that might help when he reached high school. Some of this knowledge might come back to him and be helpful in years to come.

When the evening was over, Joshua thanked his sister for the dinner and started out the door. As he was leaving, he stopped. Something was bothering him. He wasn't sure what it was. Suddenly a thought came into his mind. It was the list of the thirteen states in the sequence for ratification that his nephew had prepared in his report. It looked very familiar. Sure, he had probably seen it when he was a student. No, this was very recent in his mind.

Where had he seen that list? The only list that he had come across recently was the list Gertie had prepared for him.

He rushed back into his sister's house and asked his nephew to show him the report again.

As he looked it over, he copied the list of the states in the sequence of ratification for the constitution. Then he drove back to the office and pulled out the file on the Timpson case.

Gertie's list of unsolved homicides was right on top. He matched the two lists against each other.

The sequence in the two lists were a perfect match up to the ten states that Gertie had provided. Of course. Here was the pattern. A serial killer was going state to state and committing murders by different means.

It meant New York was next.

Jonathan checked his reference phone book and looked up the number of a precinct in New York City.

He had some acquaintance with a detective whom he knew from the time when he worked in the prosecutors office. He dialed the number.

A voice answered. "Yes, how can I help you?"

" I need to speak to Detective Wolford." said Joshua.

"Who is calling?" responded the officer on desk duty.

"Tell him it's Attorney Joshua Blaine."

"Hold on a minute."

Detective Wolford came on the phone. "Hello Blaine. What's up?" he said.

Blaine spoke: "I have some information. There is going to be a murder in New York."

Joshua realized this was quite vague and slightly ridiculous but he had to go through with this call.

Wolford answered. "What are you trying to tell me? There is a murder every day in New York.

We have many murders. Not one murder. You know that counselor. Can you tell me who is going to do it? Also where and when?"

Joshua said he didn't have that information.

Detective Wolford would have thought it was a crank call except for the fact that he knew Attorney Blaine was a level-headed person.

"Are you joking or what?" Wolford asked.

"No, I'm not kidding."

Wolford didn't know what to make of this call.

"Have you been drinking or something?" he asked.

Blaine answered. "I know it sounds ridiculous, but I'm serious. I can tell you ten different means of homicide that will not be used. Also there will be no motive for the killing." Joshua then described the information he had.

Wolford was not entirely convinced. "I can't put a APB on this limited information."

He promised to keep an eye on the matter.

Joshua could sense the skepticism on the detective's part. He didn't blame him. "I don't expect an 'All Points Bulletin'. But be aware that something is up. I thought you should know."

Joshua said goodbye, hung up the phone, sat in his chair, and wondered what he should do next.

He believed a serial killer would strike next in New York. But where? He didn't even know what city in the state would be the next target.

What could he do, if anything? He felt entirely helpless. There had to be something he could do to prevent the next murder.

The issue totally absorbed his mind as he tried to think of a solution.

The Terrorist arrived in New York City and began to organize his thoughts regarding where and how he would commit his next murder. The city has a population over 8 million people with a reputation known as the city that never sleeps. The meaning is on any day, for 24 hours, there is some place where people are working or walking. Actually there are five boroughs, but the best known is Manhattan. The others are The Bronx, Brooklyn, Queens, and Staten Island. It is Manhattan where most 24 hour activity takes place. Manhattan is very distinct from the other boroughs. Even the postal mailing addresses note the difference. A letter to any borough will be addressed as Brooklyn, New York, or Queens, New York, and similarly for the others. But Manhattan is different. A letter to Manhattan is addressed as New York, New York, not Manhatan, New York.

It was in Manhattan that the terrorist decided to continue his mayhem. He traveled around the borough using several methods for transportation. He went by bus, taxi, subway and walked around various areas. Cabs and busses were not feasible for his purpose. It would be easy to be detected or recognized by other passengers or the cabdriver The best means would be by subway. The subway system consisted of many trains traveling underground and in some areas along tracks above ground. He visited various stations at different times to see when stations were fairly deserted. As trains entered stations, he visualized how he could carry out his plan.

Mary Barker played the violin and was rehearsing at Lincoln Center. Lincoln Center was one of Manhattan's premium concert halls. Late at night, after rehearsal, Mary, as usual took the subway to ride uptown to her home. It was after 11 p.m. and the station she entered was almost deserted.

The terrorist was waiting near the front end of the platform. Mary, unwisely walked to the front of the station planning to enter one of the front cars. The front cars were usually not too crowded or as noisy as other cars. As a train approached the station, Mary moved toward the edge of the platform. The terrorist knew exactly what he planned to do. As the train neared the front where Mary stood, the terrorist, now standing behind Mary wrapped his arms around her waist and threw her into the path of the train. It happened so fast she was unable to offer any resistance. The conductor tried to slam on the brakes when he saw Mary falling on the tracks.

It was too late. The train could not stop in time. Mary had no chance.

The train struck Mary. She was killed instantly.

The train stopped, a few passengers got off when the doors opened and they approached the tragedy.

Some people standing on the platform also came over to the scene. The terrorist mingled among the crowd. Someone called 911 and screamed for police help. The terrorist slowly backed away and walked out of the station without being observed. Another murder, another success.

The news went out on police wires. Detective Wolford read the item. The report indicated that a victim was thrown off the platform in the subway by someone who apparently escaped.

Motive unknown. "Crap" said Wolford to himself. He knew that this kind of crime was not unusual in the subway. But the perpetrator was often a psycho who did not try to escape. The criminal would claim to hear voices telling him what to do or say he was acting at God's direction. This seemed different.

Wolford remembered his conversation with Joshua Blaine. He dialed Blaine and spoke to him on the phone. "Listen." he said. "We just had a homicide. Someone was thrown before a train in the subway. No motive. No apparent psycho perpetrator. It could be related to your warning. If so, I'm sorry. I feel terrible about it, but you understand there was little I could do about it. Anyway, maybe this info can help you avoid another murder."

"Thanks for calling." said Joshua. "I understand."

Joshua sat at his desk and tried to think about his next step. He looked over the list that Gertie had prepared. North Carolina was next. He had a feeling that Jean Timpson might have been right. Her husband didn't fall accidentally or commit suicide. He was pushed by a serial killer. Once again, he had a helpless feeling. What could he do?

He pulled the file that Gertie had titled "Timpson, Jean." On top in the file was the intake interview page. He had first looked it over in a cursory manner. Now he studied it carefully.

Name of client: Jean Timpson Date: July 16, 2010.

Address: 16 Peach street

Dover

Marital Status: Widow

Spouse: Stuart Timpson Occupation: Teacher

Problem: Ms. Timpson claims her husband was murdered by someone throwing him off a building.

Police believe it was a suicide. She needs help! She believes her husband was answering an ad about buying baseball cards for his collection and was meeting someone who killed him.

Possible type of case: Criminal

Joshua studied the information carefully. He picked up a pen and took a pad. He decided to create an outline profiling the killer. A profile was not 100 per cent accurate, but it was helpful.

He came up with the following regarding a serial killer:

Male, unmarried, loner, Over 21 years of age, probably in his 30's or 40's.

Physically strong, anti-American, especially against the constitution, (baseball card collector?) Probably a bigot.

He looked over what he had jotted. An idea came to him. Why did the killer use an ad about buying baseball cards? Maybe collecting baseball cards was a hobby. Was this his first victim or did it all begin in Dover, perhaps because he lived there? He came up with a plan that might bring the killer out of hiding. It was a long shot, but at this point it was the only thing he had. It might work and was worth a try.

He dialed Ms. Timpson. She answered the phone.

"Hello." she said.

"Hi. It's Joshua Blaine," he responded.

" What's up? Is anything new in the case?" she asked.

Blaine said: "Just a hunch. You said your husband was answering an ad about buying baseball cards.

Do you know where the ad appeared? Better still, do you have a copy of the ad?"

"I think I do. There is a stack of magazines that belonged to Stuart. I still have them including ones about baseball."

Joshua said "Please tear out the page of the ad if you can find it and fax it to me. Write the name of the magazine on the top of the page." he advised.

"Is this important?" she asked.

"I'm not too sure, but anyway here is my fax number." he told her.

She didn't take long to respond. She faxed the information he wanted. He looked it over. Then he called Gertie into the office.

He asked her to find a place that sold baseball collector cards. "Buy at least five hundred cards." Also, he told her he needed a copy of the magazine that Jean Timpson had named.

Gertie sensed this was about the Timpson case. She immediately got into it. A few hours later, she fulfilled Joshua's request and gave him what he asked for. Joshua looked at the material and found the phone number for ads in the magazine.

He called about placing an ad. He was in time for the next publication which came out in a few days.

He placed the ad dictating the exact wording he wanted. He supplied his credit card number for billing purposes. The ad said he had baseball cards for sale at discount prices. It pointed out that the cards came from an estate that was being liquidated. He listed his office address and phone number for response. Then he sorted the cards in alphabetical order.

He prepared a sign—in sheet, and placed it on a clipboard. Then he wrote several fictitious names on the sheet to appear as visitors to show he had many interested collectors who had come to see him.

The sign-in sheet asked for the visitor's name and address. He realized the odds were against the terrorist responding. But it was worth the chance.

Then he waited.

The first day after the ad appeared, no person came. The second day there were two visitors.

The first was a woman, about 25 years of age who said she wanted to buy some cards as a birthday gift for her husband. Obviously, she was not what Joshua was looking for. He told her to go to a baseball card dealer and to buy a set of cards instead of one or two.

The second visitor was a woman with a young son, about six or seven years old. He was interested in baseball cards. Joshua let him look at the pack and he selected five cards for purchase. The purchase made, his mother thanked Joshua and left.

A few hours later, a burly man, about 30 years old came into the office. He was clean-shaven and his hair was cut short, what was called a crew-cut. He didn't smile and actually had a surly demeanor.

Joshua asked him to sign in. He hesitated when it came to writing his name. Most people write their name without thought. He appeared to be thinking of a name to write down. To Joshua, this was significant. It was probably a phony name.

Joshua asked: "Are you looking for any specific cards?"

"I'm interested in the old Brooklyn Dodgers." he said.

Joshua answered: "Some of the old ones like Jackie Robinson and Roy Campanella are rare ones.

So are Pee Wee Reese and Duke Snider. But I'll keep my eyes open. I get additional cards all the time. I have your name and address. Let me have a phone number where I can reach you."

The visitor said, "It's hard to reach me. I'm a traveling salesman and out of town most of the time.

But I don't want Robinson or Campanella. Just white ballplayers. I'll call you."

Joshua was not surprised at the remark regarding white ballplayers. He was suspicious of this person and had a strong feeling this could be the man he was looking for. His remark indicated prejudice. No surprise there. When he left, Joshua followed him as he went to his car.

He got into a car that was parked nearby. Joshua's car was parked outside the office. As he drove away, he followed the stranger carefully, making sure he was not detected. The visitor reached a motel complex off the highway. The area was not a very busy one.

Joshua realized the address was not the one he had put on the sign-in sheet. He was either a guest, or visiting someone, or had faked the address. Joshua could not be sure. He didn't know the room number, and getting a search warrant was not possible. He copied the license plate number and noted the color and make of the car. There was not enough evidence for the police to step in. He could only watch and wait. Still, he couldn't wait forever. Joshua looked up the phone number of a private detective who had often worked for him. His name was Gordon Hanes and he picked up the phone when it rang.

"Hello" he said.

"It's Joshua Blaine. I need you to follow someone. Are you available?"

"Sure." said Gordon.

Joshua gave him the address where he was waiting. "I'm parked across the street. Can you get here soon?"

"I'll be there in about 30 minutes." said Gordon.

Joshua waited for Gordon. When he arrived, Joshua pointed to the car that he wanted followed.

He also described the man that he wanted tailed. He also warned Gordon.

"Be careful. This man could be dangerous. Very dangerous. He might be a serial killer."

Gordon said he understood. "Don't worry. I can take care of myself. But I can't keep him under 24 hour surveillance by myself. I'll need a replacement." he said.

"That's okay. I'll cover the cost." said Joshua.

Joshua left, confident he had the right man and the situation was in good hands.

It was not to be. As the cliché goes, "The best laid plans do not always work."

The motel complex had parking spots for the tenants and some spots for visitors. Usually by noon, most of the spots were empty as people went to work or for some other reason.

The terrorist's window faced the parking lot and looking out he noticed the detective's car had not moved. He was immediately suspicious. He took his M 1911 with him and approached the car. He saw the detective sitting in the front seat with no observable purpose. He walked over toward the window of the car and spoke to the detective. He asked for directions to the nearest mall. Before the detective could say anything, the terrorist pulled his gun and fired right at the detective's head. No sense taking chances thought the terrorist. Death was instant.

24 hours had passed and Joshua had not heard from the detective. He called him on the cell phone number he had. No answer. Now he was very concerned. He drove to the motel complex.

He saw the detective's car. It had not been moved. He walked over to the car and saw the horror scene.

He knew for sure he was on the track of a killer. He called Detective Wolford. Joshua spoke softly. Wolford could tell something was not good.

What's happening?" he said

"Some bad news. You probably knew retired Detective Hanes. He was doing some surveillance work for me. I just found his body. Shot in the head in his car." Joshua gave the address of the motel.

Wolford said he would be right over.

Detective Wolford arrived at the motel parking lot in a crime scene van. Joshua explained the circumstances behind the apparent murder. The motel complex consisted of a row of street level rooms with one window in each room. There was no lobby, just an office where guests would sign-in and leave a deposit for a room. The detective and Joshua headed to the office. The manager stood behind a counter and asked, "What can I do for you? I'm the manager."

Wolford flashed his badge and spoke quickly. "Do you know that someone was shot in a car in your parking lot?"

"Are you kidding?"

"No, this is no joke. I guess you heard nothing or saw anything suspicious."

"I can't believe it. I didn't see anything or hear anything. I had the TV on and I guess the sound drowned out any loud noise. You think a guest was involved."

"Pretty sure." said Wolford.

Joshua spoke up. He had noted the number on the door that the suspected terrorist had gone into.

"We would like to look into room six." Joshua said.

The manager seemed reluctant to cooperate but changed his attitude. He knew better than to antagonize the police. Besides, he knew murder was serious. " I have to tell you that the guest in room six checked out. He paid the bill." he emphasized as if it was important. He produced a key and said it opened all the rooms. Follow me he advised the police.

They opened the door to room six and began checking for anything that might have been left behind.

There was a waste can outside the room. Detective Wolford sorted through the can. Obviously, he knew how to conduct a thorough search.

"This is interesting. A holy Bible. Now why would someone throw a bible away like that."

The manager looked at the bible that Wolford held in his hand.

"We provide a bible like that in each room. They are put in each night table." the manager said. He went over to the night table and found a book in the drawer.

"Look at this book. It says 'Holy Qur'an' How did that get there? We put bibles in the drawers. Not these."

"Don't touch it. We can check it for fingerprints and DNA."

When they had finished the search, Wolford told the manager not to rent the room until further notice. He said to keep the room locked and to be sure to keep cleaning personnel out of the room.

Wolford wrapped the Qur'an in a plastic bag and told Joshua he would have it checked for prints.

Wolford called for an ambulance to take the slain detective's body. He told Joshua he would keep in touch.

Joshua drove back to the office. He sat in his office and wondered what to do next. He felt depressed.

It looked like he was back to square one. But what could he have done otherwise?

Gertie came into the office. "Anything new on the Timpson case? she asked.

"Nothing. Actually we may have let the key suspect out of our hands." Joshua responded.

"Who was that?"

"That character who came in about the baseball cards." Joshua said.

Gertie spoke. I didn't like his looks. Something about him. Just say it was my woman's instinct. I took his picture."

"What." Josh almost shouted. "You took his picture. How did you do that without his knowing about it?"

"I got this cell phone that takes pictures. It's kind of sneaky. You don't have to focus or pose for it. I was sort of playing with it. Is it important?"

Joshua replied. "Quite possibly. Let me have the picture as soon as possible."

"Of course. Give me a minute and it's yours." Gertie said.

Joshua looked at the picture. An idea came to him. Another long shot. It could help.

The phone rang. Gertie told Joshua Detective Wolford was calling. Wolford came on the phone.

"The crime lab came up with some identification from the print on the Qur'an. The suspect's print was on file, apparently from the time he was in the service. His name is Richard Worcester. I'm still worried. We know we have a serious serial killer out on the loose. I think you are right when you say he is headed to North Carolina. What can we do? I feel so helpless."

Joshua responded: "We have a few advantages. I've got an idea. We can make things difficult for him. I have his photo, and now we have his name."

"What do you have in mind? North Carolina is a big state. How can we track him down?" said Wolford.

Blaine answered. "Years ago they would put wanted pictures of criminals in post offices around the country. That practice was not too successful. We can do better. Now we can use the media to publicize the news about a dangerous serial killer on the loose."

"Do you think it will work? And will the papers and TV publicize it?" said Wolford.

Joshua answered: "This is how the media operates. It's not news until the newspapers and TV make it news. If they have a shortage of other sensational news to play up, then our story stands a good chance for coverage. Another important consideration is creditability. That's where you come in.

Obviously, a police source is taken more seriously than a call from the general public. Do you know a reporter you can get in touch with in North Carolina?"

"Yes, I do." said Wolford.

"Good. Tell the reporter there is a serial killer who has already killed eleven people over several states. Say he is headed for North Carolina. Then suggest that the reporter write about a serial killer in the state. Give them the murderer's name. I'll notify the Associated Press. They might run with the story."

The media bought into the story. It made big headlines.

A typical headline: "KILLER ON THE LOOSE."

It also received publicity on TV news.

Joshua and Wolford waited. They still had no way of preventing another murder. Perhaps someone would recognize the photograph. The odds were still long for catching the killer.

The terrorist, Richard Worcester headed for North Carolina. He purchased a ticket for a bus trip to the city of Raleigh. He liked using a bus since there was no security check, no required identification, and a rather inexpensive cost to travel. He thought how easy it would be to use an explosive to kill many passengers. He could also kill the bus driver. But either way would probably cost him his life. That was not part of his plan. Giving up his life would be the end of his jihad. Even if he survived, there would be too much publicity and a massive police hunt to track down the killer. He had to stay alive in order to continue his work. He was not sure what exactly he would do in Carolina. Surely something would come to him.

Meanwhile, Wolford and Joshua drove to North Carolina. After their arrival, they checked into a motel and waited for something to develop.

"This wait is getting on my nerves." said Wolford. "I'm sure you are right about the terrorist committing a murder in Carolina. But where or when? And we really can't prevent it in any way.

This is a real pain."

Joshua said: "I know how helpless you feel. I don't blame you. Maybe we are going about it in the wrong way. All is not lost. We can make use of the media to draw him out. He probably has a big ego. Let's contact your connections in the press. If I can be interviewed on T.V. and quoted in the newspapers, I will paint him as a stupid coward. I'll say that he is too dumb to stay free for long. I'll say that I have information that will lead to his capture very soon. We will set him up so that he will attempt to kill his next victim. We will know who the intended victim will be."

"And who would that be?" said Wolford.

"Me!" answered Joshua.

"Are you going crazy?" said Wolford.

"No. I said attempted murder. Not an actual murder." said Joshua.

"How exactly is this going to work? asked Wolford.

"I'll tell you what I have in mind. I hope it works." said Joshua.

"I hope so too. For your sake." said Wolford.

"How are you get him to try to kill you?"

" I'm going to have a heart attack." said Joshua.

"Are you kidding?" asked Wolford who was somewhat concerned.

"Well, yes and no." said Joshua. "Not a real heart attack. This killer is a head case. With all the publicity and insulting language characterizing him, I'm betting he will try to get even with me. We will tell the media that I had a heart attack and was admitted to Jefferson Memorial Hospital. Announce that I am resting in the cardiac unit. Hospitals have very little security. Their parking lots are always open to visitor parking areas. In addition, anyone can usually walk into the main entrance and ask for a pass to see someone during visiting hours as long as they know the patient's name and there are no restrictions on visiting that patient. Security is just about zero. We will get the cooperation of the police and ask to have a female detective dressed as a nurse sitting in the room where I will be in bed pretending I am a heart patient. If the plan works, the killer will try to enter my room and get his revenge.

The first part of Joshua's plan worked well. He was interviewed on local T.V. and newspaper reporters wrote stories based on interviews with Joshua. The newspaper articles and T.V. news were filled with disparaging stories about the stupidity and immorality of the terrorist.

Richard Worcester's name was given wide publicity. Joshua's plan was coordinated with the local police?"

The terrorist was angry. He learned about Joshua's remarks and felt insulted. It was time to teach Joshua Blaine a lesson. He would pay for his disrespect. What could be better? He would get rid of Blaine and at the same time commit Jihad in North Carolina. Wonderful, he thought to himself.

The terrorist drove to the hospital and parked the car in the hospital parking area. He knew that hospitals had an open door policy. There was no security at the entrance and anyone could enter without a problem. But getting to Blaine might be dangerous. No. He was not stupid. He needed to get to Blaine without any suspicion. He figured out a way to get to the cardiac room where Blaine was under observation. It would be easy to carry out his jihad.

The receptionist at the desk received a call from one of the staff physicians. He told her to be on the lookout for a patient who would left the floor without permission.

It was about 4 P. M. and the terrorist knew that it was the time when most workers went off duty and the new shift would be entering the building. He was looking for a male who be close to his physique and resemble him slightly. Finally he saw someone waiting at a bus stop outside the hospital.

The man's appearance met the terrorist's needs. He drove quickly to the bus stop and came abreast to the man who was dressed in a blue hospital outfit with a name tag over his heart.

"Excuse me. I've lost my way. I'm looking for a super market." the terrorist said.

"Perhaps you can help me find one. By the way, do you need a lift?"

"Sure. Thanks." answered the man waiting at the bus stop. He got into the car and the terrorist drove quickly away. The car headed to the highway and eventually drove off into a wooded area. He stopped the car. "Why are we stopping?" asked the passenger.

The terrorist pulled his gun out and pointed it at his passenger. "Listen, you won't get hurt. I need your clothes. Take yours off and exchange them with mine."

The passenger disrobed and the terrorist took his clothing. The terrorist then pulled a knife out and stabbed the man until he was sure that he was dead. Then he dragged the body into a deserted bush area and hid the body as best he could. He quickly dressed into the hospital outfit and drove back to the hospital.

As soon as he entered the hospital, he was seen by the receptionist. She quickly called security and reported a problem. The terrorist rang for the elevator and waited for door to open for the upper floors. When the elevator door opened, two burly security men grabbed him, wrestled him to the floor, and put him in a strait jacket.

The terrorist was surprised and unable to offer any resistance. He was taken to the psychiatric ward. In the cardiac unit, the detective nurse received a call on her cell phone. She was told about the attempt to enter the hospital by an unauthorized person. Jason was told about the call. He immediately made a possible connection to the terrorist. After learning where the man was being held, he went to the psychiatric ward with Wolford who had been waiting outside the ward.

Wolford flashed his badge in order to gain entrance.

"That's him." shouted Joshua when he saw the terrorist. "We have our man."

Wolford put him in handcuffs and called for the police to take him away.

Joshua and Wolford watched as the terrorist was put into the police van.

A detective standing by said, "We found the body of the murdered patient. That was good police work.

How did you get on to him?"

"Well, let's just say the holy book gave us his identity." said Joshua.

"The Bible?" replied the detective.

" Not the bible, but the Holy Qur'an." said Joshua.

"Also, a ten year old doing his homework." said Joshua.

"It sounds so weird,' said the detective.

Joshua answered. "I'll tell you how weird it is. Of all the people who he tried to disguise himself as, he picks an escapee from the psychiatric ward. It was easy to identify him because he wore the blue outfit of a psychiatric patient. He believed that the constitution and our government limited his freedom. After his trial, he will be six feet under or in prison for life. And then he will know what it is to live without freedom."

" Now, that's ironic." said Wolford.

"I have to leave now" said Joshua.

"Why are you going in such a hurry? asked Wolford.

"I have to see the woman who started me on this case and give her the news that we caught the man who killed her husband." said Joshua.

"Why don't you call her?"

"No. I want to see her personally. I'm hoping to see her more than once." said Joshua.

"Good Luck. I would say she is a lucky woman." smiled Wolford.

SURPRISE

Henry Wilson was a loser. Not just a loser but a guy who always seemed to have hard luck follow him. If he needed a break, it was sure things would never go his way. Now, he was twenty two years old, about 5'11" and not too bad looking. Things started to go bad for him when he was 17 years old.

He was hanging around the local candy store with his friends, which was a normal activity in the Bronx.

The so-called activity was nothing more than looking at girls as they passed by or arguing about some baseball issue. Who was better, Mantle, Mays, or Snider and were the Yankees better than the Giants or Brooklyn? You never called them the Dodgers, just Brooklyn. And Brooklyn might just as well have been in another country. Everybody seemed to hate Brooklyn the most. In fact, you would never date a girl from Brooklyn. The trip was considered too far from the Bronx. As for the Giants or Yankees, you never used the words New York, just Giants or Yankees.

The guys who hung around the corner candy store included all kinds of characters. There was the baseball expert, an expert only in his own mind. Then there was the expert on women. If a girl passed by with big boobs, the expert would offer his advice. Stay away from her. If you marry her, you will wind up with a wife with a big behind. Yes, big boobs meant a big behind in the future. Where did this knowledge come from? Nobody knew. Besides, who was even thinking of marriage at that stage.

Still the expert would offer his opinion without being asked. Since he knew so much, he was called the expert. Most guys had nicknames. You were never known by the name on your birth certificate.

If you were overweight, you were known as Fats, Fatso, Fatty or Chubby. If you were thin, you were called Slim. If you had lots of hair on your head and always looked like you needed a haircut, you were the Mop. The important thing about dating girls was getting laid. Even if you didn't go all the way with your date, you could brag and lie about it saying you made out 100%.

Henry Wilson had one thing that was very valuable. He had a car. One of the boys on the block asked him for a ride to the local deli. Henry, always the nice guy agreed to provide the ride. When they reached the Deli, his friend went in and came out a few minutes later.

"Let's get going. I bought a half gallon of ice cream and it will melt quickly," Henry's friend said.

They drove a few blocks away when suddenly a police siren forced them to stop. The next thing Henry knew was that he was under arrest and in handcuffs along with his friend.

A robbery had taken place at the deli and Henry was charged with aiding and abetting the crime.

The police told him it meant a charge of third-degree robbery. Even worse for Henry was that a few weeks ago, he reached the age of 17 years. That meant he would not be charged in Juvenile Court. In Juvenile Court convictions were treated more leniently than regular court and if convicted, the punishment could be serving time in a juvenile prison, not in an adult prison. Also, he would not have a criminal record. But Henry the loser missed out by a few weeks after reaching his seventeenth birthday.

At the arraignment, the magistrate read the complaint filed by the police. He asked Henry if he had driven the car after the robbery. Henry started to say he had nothing to do with the robbery, but the Judge cut him off.

"This is not the place to hear your argument about guilt or innocence. In fact you have the right to remain silent and anything you say against yourself can be used against you. You have the right to have an attorney represent you. Do you have an attorney?"

"No." said Henry

"Can you afford one?"

Henry again answered he did not.

"Then I will assign one for you. Bail is set at $10,000."

Henry couldn't make the bail price and was sent to jail to await meeting his court appointed attorney.

After a restless night, the following morning Henry met his court appointed attorney.

The attorney introduced himself. Most court appointed attorneys were recent law school graduates or attorneys who were not too successful in criminal practice.

The attorney told Henry he would try to negotiate a plea deal with the prosecutor's office. If Henry insisted on going to trial, a guilty verdict would probably lead to a prison sentence of five to ten years. Besides, his friend might make a deal and implicate Henry in order to get a lighter sentence for himself. He said he might be able to negotiate a guilty plea in exchange for probation. It would mean no time in prison. But Henry would have to admit to committing the crime. The attorney did not tell Henry that a guilty plea in exchange for probation meant freedom from prison but carried a criminal record. The prosecutor offered the deal. The attorney advised Henry to accept it. Henry agreed to the deal and the judge agreed to set the sentence. Henry was free from serving time in prison but he had a criminal record.

Life as a free man with a criminal record was a hardship. It was difficult to get any kind of decent job. The only thing that seemed to go well for Henry was that he began dating a neighborhood girl whom he liked. Her name was Gloria and Henry knew her from the time they were teen-agers. After a short courtship, they were married by a judge. Henry drifted into various jobs. He worked bagging groceries at a local supermarket. Gloria got a job as a salesperson at a local clothing store. They moved into a rent controlled apartment and made ends meet. However, Henry was fed up with his job.

He didn't like the work and he finally quit and got a job flipping hamburgers at a fast food chain.

Henry was not content with the way his life was going. He hated the work and decided there had to be easier ways to make money. He decided he was too smart for these menial jobs that paid very little.

He believed his brain could be put to better use. The path he took would lead to momentous consequences.

First he began pick pocketing. To be safe and avoid detection, he worked among crowds where the victim was off guard. He used the subways during rush hours. Swarms of people rushed into the trains and brushed against each other. It was easy to collide with a person and swipe a wallet out of a back pocket at the same time. It was not hard to do. He also worked at parades. As crowds lined the sidewalks, Henry would brush up against a parade watcher and swipe a wallet from a back pocket, but there was not much profit in it for Henry. There was also the danger of an arrest by a police officer.

Besides, parades were not held too often.

He came up with another scheme. He went into a restaurant and ordered a dessert and coffee.

When a group left a table, Henry would note that a tip was left for the waiter. Pretending to go to the rest room, he came abreast of the targeted table and bent down as if he had dropped something. If he saw a ten dollar bill on the table he would quickly snatch it and put it in his pocket and replace it with five dollar bill.

A twenty dollar tip would be replaced with a ten dollar bill. He called it his 50% plan. The waiter could only complain about the size of the tip. But he began to run out of restaurants and he worried that he would arouse suspicions. He needed another scheme.

One night on TV news, he watched a story about a celebrity cheating on his wife. Henry knew that spousal cheating was not uncommon. He came up with another plan to make some money. There were motels that rented rooms for a few hours at so-called day rates.

These rentals were used by couples having illicit sex, usually cheating on a spouse. Henry drove to one of the motels and watched from a spot in the parking lot. When a couple left in two cars without any luggage, he assumed they were having a sexual affair. Henry snapped a picture of the couple as they left the motel. He followed the male driver as he drove away. When the driver parked, Henry quickly walked up to him.

"Just a minute." he said. "I know you were cheating with my wife. I've taken your picture as you left.

I'm not looking to cause too much trouble. If you promise not to see my wife again, I'll let you have the photo I took of you and my wife when you left the motel. That will be the end of it. I've also been out of work and am hard up for money. This is not an attempt at blackmail. But maybe you can help me out a little." The man was usually shaken up and couldn't think straight. The ruse worked for a time and Henry was making some decent money. Then came the big shock and surprise. Something he never figured could occur.

One day Henry was parked in one of the cheap motels when a couple began to leave. He looked at the woman several times to make sure he was seeing things correctly.

"Holy shit," he said to himself. "I can't believe this." What he saw was Gloria, his wife leaving the motel along with another man. He drove home and said nothing to his wife about the incident. All day he was filled with rage. He was ready to explode any moment.

Gloria could see something was bothering Henry. "What's the matter?" she said.

He screamed at her. "You're a bitch and I'm not an idiot." he shouted at her. Then he grabbed her throat and began choking her. She screamed for help. A neighbor called 911 when he heard the screams.

The police arrived but it was too late to save her. Henry was arrested. At the police station a detective questioned Henry.

"Why did you kill her?" he was asked.

"She was cheating on me." said Henry.

"Tell me about it." the detective asked.

Henry told the detective about the motel incident and seeing his wife leaving with another man.

He named the motel, and the time and date of what he saw. The detective left with the information and began to type a statement in the form of a confession that he assumed Henry would sign. He also made a call to the motel.

Later, he came back to Henry who was waiting in another room.

"Did you know that your wife worked as a desk clerk in that motel?" said the detective.

"What! Are you kidding me?"

"No. It's the truth. I just checked it out with the motel. I guess she didn't want you to know she worked in such a sleazy place. What you probably saw was her leaving after work with the manager.

That's why they left in two cars. You jumped to the wrong conclusion. She should not have been killed."

Henry was shocked. He knew he was going to prison for a long time. The loser's losing streak was continuing.

SCHOOL

The opening day of school is usually an exciting event. Students form little groups and greet each other after the summer recess. Some hug each other, some kiss, others shake hands. It is more exciting for a new teacher to the school, especially one beginning a first day as a teacher.

Brian Wilson was excited and somewhat nervous. He gently pushed his way through the throng of students and reached the front entrance. An adult woman stood in his path.

"Can I help you? she asked.

"Yes. I have a letter introducing me to the principal." He showed the letter to her and she glanced at it and opened the door allowing him to enter.

"Go straight inside and make a right turn. You will see the door marked principal."

Brian entered and following directions came to the principal's office. He entered and was met by a secretary who asked if she could help him.

He showed her the letter and she took it into the inner office. She came out in a few minutes.

"Please take a seat. Mr. Rabin will see you soon."

Brian sat down and wondered if the principal was really busy or wanted to appear busy.

After about ten minutes, the secretary picked up an inter-com phone and apparently was told to send the visitor in.

He entered the principal's office and was told to have a seat. The principal didn't offer a hand shake and didn't appear particularly warm. He glanced at Brian's resume and then spoke quickly.

"Welcome to our school. You will receive your program in room 350. See Mrs. Callon there. She is the head of your department. We expect you to carefully follow our directions which are distributed in a weekly calendar. Subject matter material and teaching policies will be explained by Mrs. Callon.

I expect bell to bell teaching along with a carefully organized lesson plan for each class. Good Luck!"

It was so matter of fact that it seemed like a carefully rehearsed speech repeated by rote.

Brian headed up to the third floor and found room 350. Mrs Callon was seated at a desk in the office.

She arose when he entered and said, "Mr. Wilson?"

"Yes," he answered.

"Glad to have you aboard. I've made out your program. You will be teaching in room 324. I was able to program your five classes in the same room for you. Here are the keys for the room and closets. If you have any problems or questions, feel free to ask for help. I know this is your first teaching job, so I will ask a volunteer to act as a mentor. In addition, you are welcome to observe me teaching my classes. I'm supposed to be the expert, " she said with a smile.

She seemed so sincere and pleasant and Brian noticed the difference between her and his meeting with the principal.

Brian walked over to room 324 and found the room occupied by an elderly gentleman who was emptying the desk drawers by taking out personal items.

"Welcome," he said and offered a handshake. "I'm Jim Taylor. I'm retiring. 35 years in this school system is enough. Is this your first job teaching?"

"Yes." said Brian.

"Well here is my advice. Never argue with the principal, even if he doesn't know what the hell he is talking about. Just yes him to death. He has all the power on his side and can make things difficult for you.

You will also get a lot of nonsense about how to improve teaching. Everybody is an expert, especially college professors and politicians. Teachers are the fall guys. I'll sum it up for you. In order for students to succeed, you need students who are able to learn and want to learn. Everything else is in second place if you don't have those two things. I have kept a list of the recommended solutions offered by so-called experts over the years. Maybe you can use it. If nothing else, it might help you keep your sanity when teachers get blamed for all the problems in education.

Here, keep the list or throw it away. I have no further use for it." He then handed a card to Brian with a list headed "So-called solutions." The numbered items appeared as follows:

1. Better teachers
2. Smaller classes
3. Better textbooks
4. Higher teacher pay
5. Better teacher training
6. More education courses in college
7. Evaluation of teachers based on student test scores
8. Integration of schools, especially racial integration
9. More teacher time in teaching
10. Longer school year
11. Longer school day
12. Homogeneous classes
13. Heterogeneous classes
14. Charter schools
15. Better training of administrators (Principals, Assistant Principals)
16. More healthful food in lunchroom
17. Abolish last in first out for layoffs
18. End power of teacher unions
19. Limit or end collective bargaining
20. Mandate uniforms for student dress code

Mr. Taylor then spoke to Brian. "You may think I'm too cynical. But remember my first adage.

The most important factor is the student. I repeat. You need students who want to learn and are able to learn. I call it the Casey Stengel syndrome. Remember Casey. As manager of the New York Yankees he won five consecutive world championships from 1949 to 1954. Then he became manager of the New York Mets in 1962 and the team lost 120 games. That still stands as the record for most losses in a season by a major league team. What changed? The players changed. Without top athletes poor Casey was a loser. The analogy is the same for teachers. You need to have capable students. Some on my list for so-called solutions will work sometimes. Some will never work. Again, it depends on the student more than anything else. Remember that the students come with a lot of extra baggage created outside the classroom. That's all you need to know."

As Mr. Taylor finished packing his belongings, he shook Brian's hand again and wished him good luck.

When Brian was left alone in the room he wondered if he would become as cynical as Mr. Taylor after he was teaching many years.

The first few weeks of teaching were uneventful. Brian felt overworked teaching five classes each day and preparing lesson plans for each class. Another time consuming chore was preparing tests and then marking each test paper. He wondered about critics who said teachers didn't work a full day.

They had no idea about a teacher's work beyond the school day. Brian often stayed after school trying to assess the day's work in class. The school was quiet and most of the staff usually had left for the day.

Brian was alone on the third floor and the school was almost entirely deserted. After about an hour of work, Brian was tired and felt it was time to leave. Instead of taking the elevator, he decided to walk down the stairway. He pushed the door leading to the steps, but the door would not open easily.

Something seemed to prevent the door from opening fully. The door was slightly ajar. Maybe the door was broken.

As Brian was about to leave and go to another stairway, he happened to glance at the slight opening at the door. He couldn't believe what he saw. It looked like a human hand was extended on the floor.

He grabbed his cell phone and called the office.

He asked for security. He said it was an emergency and he needed immediate help. In a few minutes, two men from the security force in the school came to the scene. The door to the stairway was pushed open. On the floor in a pool of blood was the principal, Mr. Rabin. The security officer, Mr. Thomas checked for a pulse.

He spoke. "No pulse. He's dead." He turned him over on his back. "Look! There's a knife sticking out of his stomach. Christ! He's been murdered. Call the police. I can't believe this." Neither could Brian.

Who said teaching was dull?

Two detectives came to the school. The lead detective was John Munson and the other was Charles Owens. They questioned Thomas the security officer who had found the body.

"Do you know how many people were in the building?" Munson asked. "Not exactly. There are about 3500 students enrolled here. Anyone could stay and actually keep hidden in some room if they wish. In addition, parents can easily enter the building if someone leaves a door unlocked. Some teachers stay late. There are about 180 teachers on staff. Then there's the custodial staff. We also have office workers and some administrators who might stay late. Even though we have security staff on duty, it is possible for an intruder to sneak into the building."

"Great! We have thousands of possible suspects." said Owens somewhat sarcastically.

"Tell me who was definitely in the building."

"Well, the principal's secretary can tell you when she saw Mr. Rabin last. The custodial staff work cleaning out the rooms. The basketball team was practicing in the gym. Of course, Mr. Wilson was here. He first saw the body and called us. We had a security detail of three officers, including me."

Detective Owens had been questioning the secretary, Ms. Sweeter who had not left the building.

He said that she told him that she worked until 5 o'clock. Mr. Rabin had left the office about 4:15 to make the rounds. She said he often did this at the end of the day.

Detective Munson asked Brian when he first saw the body. Brian told him it was about 5:00 o'clock when he left. That meant Mr. Rabin had been killed between 4:15 and 5 P.M.

Munson called for the custodial worker who had worked on the third floor.

When the custodial worker arrived, Munson questioned him.

His name was Phil Landy. "Just call me Phil. That's what everyone calls me."

"Tell me what you do, Phil." said Munson.

"I sweep each room on the third floor. I empty the waste baskets. I make sure the windows are closed.

Then I wash the boards unless the teacher leaves a not to erase message on the board."

"Was there anything unusual in any of the rooms?" asked Munson.

"No. All the rooms seemed the same to me." said Phil.

"What time do you work on the third floor?"

"I start after 3:30."

"Did you see or hear anything unusual on the floor?

"No, everything seemed the same."

"Okay. That's all for now. Thanks for your help."

Munson then spoke to the security chief.

"Who else could have been in the building?" Munson asked the security person.

"The basketball team was practicing in the gym. They are probably still there."

Please call the coach and have him call me on my cell phone number."

"I can do that." answered the security chief.

When the coach reached Detective Munson, he was asked to notify the players to report to Munson at an office room that had been set aside for Munson to use for his investigation.

After most of the players arrived, Munson asked if anyone had seen or heard anything that seemed suspicious when they left after practice.

None responded.

"Did anyone go to the third floor? asked Munson.

William Harris, a tall center raised his hand.

"What were you doing on the third floor?" asked Munson.

"I forgot my book bag and I remembered that I must have left it in my last class. That's in room 328."

"What time were you in room 328?"

"It must have been about 4:30, after practice. I left about 15 minutes later.

"What were you doing for 15 minutes in that room?"

"The homework assignment for the next day was on the board and I copied it."

Detective Munson then told the Security chief that he wanted to meet with the faculty the next morning when the staff came to school. He said he would address them in the auditorium.

The next morning the staff arrived and took seats in the auditorium. By now, the word had got around that Mr. Rabin had been stabbed and was dead. You could feel the anxiety among the teachers. How safe was the school was a refrain frequently heard.

Detective Owens spoke to Munson. "This is a hell of a case. We have thousands of suspects.

Teachers, administrators, students, parents, office workers, custodial workers, intruders, even part of the security staff. Anyone could have done it. We haven't got a good clue."

"That's true, but au contraire. I have a suspicion who did it."

"How is that?" said Owens.

"It's a matter of homework." said Munson.

This I have to see" said Owens.

Munson then spoke to the staff from the stage. He assured the staff that they were not in any danger.

Police would be stationed around each floor.

Owens thought to himself and hoped Munson was right about safety in the school.

Munson asked security who taught in room 328 at the end of the day.

"That would be Mr. Billings."

"Ask Mr. Billings to see me after this meeting."

After the meeting ended in the auditorium, Mr. Billings came to the room where Munson was waiting.

Munson asked Billings to tell him what time he left the building.

"I left at 3:30 after my last class." said Billings.

Munson became very serious in his tone. "Mr. Billings. I am going to arrest you for suspicion of murder." He then announced the four parts of the Miranda warning. Billings seemed startled.

"Are you serious? " said Billings.

"Yes, I am. You have not told me the truth. You were in the building after 4:15." said Munson.

"How can you say that?" said Billings.

"Easy! You put the homework on the board for the next day. And that was done after 4 o'clock."

"How do you know that?" said Billings.

"Well I know that the custodial worker washed the board. That was after 4 P.M. You had a compulsion to put the homework on the board for the next day. One of your students came back to the room and saw the homework on the board. He said it was not there at the end of class. His testimony and the custodial worker will verify that the homework had to be written on the board after 4 P.M. That means you are not truthful about the time you left the building. You were on the third floor and obviously wanted to keep that fact hidden. You were in a position to murder Mr. Rabin. That is why you are being arrested."

Munson reached for his handcuffs and cuffed Billings. Then he led him down the same staircase where the homicide had taken place.

Owens was impressed. He thought to himself.

How ironic! Who said homework was not impotant?